Other books by Lynn Blake John

REVENGE OF THE VEGETABLES

THE ACCIDENTAL ATHLETE

DIAL Y LLYSIAU

THE ANIMAL CHRONICLES

LYNN BLAKE JOHN

ISBN-13: 978-1502785862

ISBN-10: 1502785862

SQUIGGLES PRESS
Carmarthen, Wales

For Simon Glyndwr John

A huge thank you to Andrea Blake, Donna Linse, Di Schonhut, Sherry Owen, Barbara Youssefi Davis, Beau Riffenburgh and Doris Lee for all their help and support.

TABLE OF CONTENTS

SOLO FLIGHT

'We're going on a trip,' said Hattie Hummingbird's mother.

'Where are we going?' asked Hattie.

'Panama,' said her mum.

'Panama? Where's that?'

'It's a country in Central America about three

thousand miles from here.'

'I don't want to go,' said Hattie. 'I'll stay here.'

'I'm sorry, Hattie, but that's impossible. We're ruby-throated hummingbirds and every winter we fly to a nice, warm place so we can drink the nectar from lovely flowers and eat plump, tasty insects.'

'I don't care. I'd miss all my friends. I want to stay here.'

'Hattie, everyone has to leave because the days are growing shorter and there won't be anything to eat here up North.'

'What about school? I was going to join the nest building club.'

'Don't worry, Hattie, we'll come back here in the spring.'

'Oh, all right, Mum. But I'm not looking forward to it.'

'Hattie, where's your sense of adventure?' said her older brother, Hugo, who overheard the conversation. 'You're going to see many new places and meet many new hummingbirds.'

Hattie was sulking and didn't bother answering Hugo.

The next day Hattie, Hugo and their mum started to prepare for the journey. They gorged themselves on some luscious spiders, gnats, bees, and ants with a few aphids for good measure. They drank some nectar from some late flowering bee balms, lupines and hollyhocks.

'I'm stuffed,' said Hattie.

'Eat up,' encouraged Hugo. 'You'll need that nourishment for the trip. Did you know, Hattie, that our cousins, the Rufous hummingbirds, fly all the way from Alaska to Mexico? Boy, do they gobble mosquitoes.'

The day finally came for the hummingbirds to start their migration. Mum suddenly told Hattie, 'We're not going together. You're on your own.'

'Whaaaaaat? What do you mean, "I'm on my own"?'

'We have to fly separately,' said Hugo. 'If we're in a big group, we can be spotted and then we're easy prey for cats or lizards or bats or snakes.'

'Ooooo, I hate snakes,' said Hattie. 'But how will I know where to go?'

'It just happens,' said Mum. 'We follow the same fly zone every year.'

'I don't believe you, Mum. I feel a panic attack coming on.'

Mum didn't answer Hattie. Instead, she gave her a hug and a gentle push and Hattie set off on her journey. She flew west from Canada across the United States towards Central America. Food along the way was plentiful thanks to the nectar of the flowering spotted jewelweed. She had some good night's sleep thanks to the torpor that slowed down her heart and breathing.

After a few weeks of flying Hattie saw something eerie in the distance.

'Oh my goodness, what is that gigantic body of water? Nobody warned me about this. I can't even swim. And I certainly don't see any hummingbird helicopters.'

Below her was the Gulf of Mexico, five hundred miles of water to cross before she could reach land again.

Hattie stopped abruptly. The Gulf was very scary. She glanced around and saw some shrimp fishermen and some oil rigs but nothing much else. Not a single McBird restaurant in sight.

All of a sudden a speck appeared in the sky. As it grew larger Hattie realised it was another hummingbird.

Henry Hummingbird waved hello. 'I'm Henry. I'm off to Panama. Is this your first time?'

'Yes. I don't see how I can possibly fly over this water.'

'You're right, the Gulf is daunting and frightening. All of us hummingbirds find it a challenge and, to be quite honest, some of us don't make it. You'll feel tired, you'll feel hungry, you'll despair and you'll want to give up. There might be terrible storms. I always try to remind myself: When the going gets tough, the tough keep flying.'

Hattie said goodbye and soared into the bright,

blue sky.

A few hours into the flight the sky turned grey and it began to rain. At first the rain was just a sprinkling but then the rain turned fierce. It swirled and whirled and the wind came up. It blew Hattie left and right and upside down and backwards. Then the storm turned into a hurricane! Hattie was more terrified than she had ever been in her whole life.

'What did Henry say?' she asked herself. "When the going gets tough, the tough keep flying.' I've got to hold on to my courage and picture the sunlit shore.'

Though she could barely flap her wings she kept flying through the storm and the dark night, battered by the water and the shrieking winds. She kept repeating, 'the tough keep flying, the tough keep flying, the tough keep flying.'

At dawn the Gulf Coast appeared on the horizon

and Hattie breathed a huge sigh of relief. After she landed she spotted Henry resting on a bright red Turk's cap flower.

'Boy, am I starved,' said Hattie after her twenty-two hour trip to the other side. 'Let's eat.'

After a drink of flower nectar and some prime flies, Hattie and Henry were ready to fly to their final wintering destination in Panama.

Henry said, 'It was nice getting to know you, Hattie. I hope we can meet up in the spring when we go back home. You were very brave during that storm. I'll be looking for a mate and I think you would make a wonderful mother.'

Hattie was very flattered.

'I'll look forward to it. I was very frightened at the start of the migration but after flying through the hurricane I have a lot more confidence. I won't be afraid of the journey home to our breeding ground.'

'See you there,' she added, after swallowing an exceptionally tasty beetle.

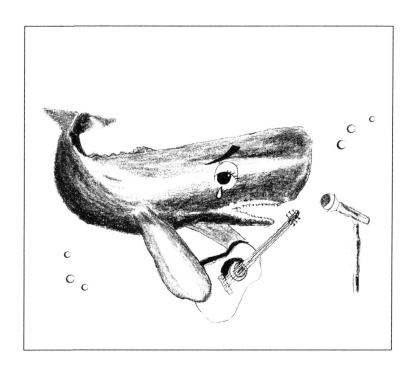

TOP OF THE POPS

Waldo Whale said to his brother, William, 'You know that I've always loved singing. Now I've decided to make it my career.'

'Come on, Waldo, be realistic. It's so hard to make a name for yourself in pop music. Look how hard Wilson Whale tried. Even though he had a top ten single, his career never really got going. Why don't you just take over the family business and fish for plankton?'

'I won't make the same mistakes as Wilson. I won't be a one-hit wonder. As well as singing the old standbys, I've written some new songs.'

'OK, clever clogs, let me hear one.'

Follow me
Across the sea
Across the ocean
Forward motion.

Through waters deep
I shall never sleep
No more Krill stew
If I don't find you.

Hear my low frequency sounds
In the cold feeding grounds
I shall lose control
When I see your blow hole.

You are my one true love
You, I am in awe of
I shall search forever
Now and whatever.

'Well, actually, that's pretty nice. But if we live to be ninety years old, do you think you will still feel like performing?'

'I'll never give it up,' answered Waldo.

Actually, what Waldo meant was that he would never give up Winifred Whale. He met her during a long migration but Waldo went off with his pod and Winifred went off with hers. Yet he was dazzled by her graceful fluke tail and he couldn't put her out of his mind. He hoped and prayed that she would recognise his call if he could broadcast some pop songs through the ocean waves.

The next day Waldo sent in a demo tape to "Underwater X Factor." Amazingly, by return of echolocation he learned that he would be performing on the next show. He was extremely nervous since he had never sung in public before. His devoted Mum encouraged him.

'Waldo, I know you're scared but just do your best. The entire pod is behind you. No matter what happens, we will still love you.'

'Thanks, Mum,' said a nervous Waldo as he swam to the surface and took a deep breath through his blow holes. Winning the competition meant everything to Waldo.

The first contestant on stage was Wilson Whale. What a surprise! Everyone knew that Wilson was very talented but no one ever expected to see him again. Wilson sang his song:

> I've been to the heights
> I've been to the depths
> I was top of the tree
> Then my fans left me.

I sang my song
I got it wrong
My heart bled
My career was dead.

So then I roamed
Far from home
Under oceans deep
Twenty-five hundred feet.

But now I'm back
I hope, on track
Humility
Not futility.

Wilson's song was so touching and poignant. Waldo shed a tear or two, just like the rest of the audience. They saw how much he had suffered with the downturn to his fortunes.

Waldo and the eight other finalists sang their songs. But Wilson's clear voice soared above them all.

Waldo said to Mum, 'I wanted to win so badly but we all felt that Wilson's song had a haunting and true, whale-like quality to it. Besides, his voice was greater than 188 decibels and louder than a jet plane taking off. I'm going home but I'm going to try again next year.'

Waldo kept up a brave face but he still desperately wanted to find Winifred. He tried one more time:

> Hear me, Winifred
> My love is unlimited
> Hear my plaintive song
> I sing it all day long.
>
> When you hear my sound
> Go to our breeding ground
> Will you be my mate
> Can we procreate?

Waldo's song travelled 10,000 miles across the oceans. Winifred heard it! She couldn't answer back because female whales don't have a loud voice. But she swam from Antarctica to the breeding grounds near the Equator.

'Waldo, I remember you from last year's

migration. I saw the twinkle in your eye. Your songs are lovely. I think you're a wonderful, strong whale and I'd be lucky to be your mate.'

Waldo was overjoyed. 'I'll do anything I can to make you happy, Winifred.'

Waldo and Winifred sang a song together:

> We met across the ocean
> What a strange notion
> We decided to mate
> It must have been fate.
>
> Our baby is called, "Wayne"
> He sleeps on one side of his brain
> He weighed six tons at birth
> That's a normal girth.
>
> His tail propels him
> His flippers steer him
> Plenty of blubber
> To keep warm in chilly water.
>
> Waldo wanted stardom
> It would have been awesome
> But a family is much better
> This is our love letter.

THE BEE WHO WAS AFRAID OF FLOWERS

Betty the little bee sat in her cell in the beehive.

'I don't want to do it,' said Betty.

17

'But, Betty, you know it's time,' said Winifred the worker bee.

'I don't want to leave the hive. It's cozy and warm in here.'

'Now, Betty, don't you remember that when you were a baby, I came back from the flowers with nectar and pollen to feed you? Well, now it's your turn to help feed our young bees.'

'I don't care, I tell you. I can't do it. Why aren't you listening to me?' cried Betty.

Winifred asked, 'What's really worrying you, Betty?'

Betty thought about it for a moment.

'For one thing, those tulip petals are so big that they might smother me when I drink their nectar. Second, you know I'm afraid of heights and drinking the nectar from apple blossoms might make me faint and fall to the ground. And third, I'm worried that when I fly deep inside a lily, I'll be trapped and won't be able make my way back up and out into the air.'

'But, Betty, how do you know these things will happen to you if you never even try?'

'I just know it,' Betty insisted stubbornly. 'And, furthermore, how do I know I will ever find my way back to the hive? I might even be eaten by a bear along the way. Or a human might spray me with a bug killer and I'll be dead. Those humans think that I want to sting them. All I really want is to get out of their way.'

'What about all the plants which won't bear fruit if we don't pollinate them?' asked Winifred. 'The world needs us bees to help make food. Think about a world if there were no apples or cherries or peaches or strawberries or beans or peas or broccoli or cucumbers . . . '

Nothing Winifred could say would convince Betty to change her mind.

Betty spent a sleepless night worrying about all the things that could go wrong when she flew near flowers. She felt guilty, too, because the thousands of young bees were hungry and she didn't want them to starve.

The next morning Shirley, the old Scout bee, said to Betty, 'Come with me when I look for flowers.'

'But . . . I don't . . . I can't . . .'

'Stick with me. My waggle dance will point you to the flowers and I'll make sure you get home safely.'

Reluctantly, Betty followed Shirley into the gardens.

'Betty . . . Betty . . . Betty . . .' A golden sunflower seemed to call her name. Betty just couldn't resist the scent and lovely colour.   She ventured into the sunflower and lapped up the nectar with her proboscis - her long tongue - while pollen stuck to her legs.

Betty buzzed from flower to flower, drinking nectar and spreading pollen.   Then she spotted a beautiful copper butterfly sitting nearby on a daisy.

'I'm enjoying the sunshine,' said Bertha the butterfly. 'But in my heart I'm very lonely.'

'Why are you lonely?' enquired Betty.

'You live in a colony with many friends and family but I'm out here on my own. We butterflies work alone.'

'That must be hard,' Betty said. 'You don't have anyone to help you when you are afraid.'

Betty flew on to some cornflowers and then she drank the nectar from some asters and lavender. Suddenly her honey tummy sac felt full so she flew

21

back towards the hive. Shirley buzzed past her but Betty just waved; she didn't need any help finding home. She didn't even worry if she would find it or not.

'Winifred, I'm back,' she said. 'I didn't even need to ask Shirley to show me the way to the hive.'

'I knew you could do it, Betty,' said Winifred.

Winifred showed her how to give her nectar to Hannah, a hive bee, whose stomach changed the nectar into honey. Hannah stored the honey in a honeycomb.

Hannah said, 'This honey will feed the newborn larvae and the other bees over the winter.'

Betty tickled the tummies of the larvae she was feeding.

'These babies are so cute but so helpless. They really need me.'

'I'm proud of you,' said Winifred. 'You faced your fears and you got past them.'

'It wasn't so bad,' Betty discovered. 'I was scared but once Scout Shirley showed me the sunflowers, I managed just fine. I feel like a different honeybee. It's feels good to help others and not worry so much about myself. I need to go back to work now, Winifred.'

'See you later, Betty.'

Betty flew back to the gardens. She made hundreds of trips to and from the hive that day. The bees would have plenty of honey to see them through the winter.

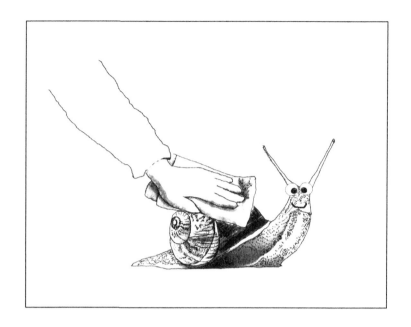

THE SNAIL'S TALE

Sheldon the Snail was very proud. He had been
chosen to be the ambassador of the "Slow Movement,"
the crusade to hit the brakes on life's hectic pace. This
morning he had been taken in a stretch limo for a
photo shoot because, obviously, he couldn't slither

there fast enough.

'Sheldon, darling, we're delighted to see you.'

'On behalf of my entire gastropod family, I'd like to say that I'm honoured to be here.'

'Would you like some plant stems or some decayed leaves before we start?'

'Lovely.'

After a quick munch, Sheldon got ready for photographs. Philippa, the photographer's assistant, shined up his shell. She said to Sheldon, 'Sheldon, you're so lucky to own your own home. The cost of housing in this country is ridiculous and I don't know when I'll ever be able to afford a house.'

'Yes, I am lucky, Philippa, but my house does need some updating. I don't have central heating so in the winter I have to hibernate and in the summer, if there is a drought, I have to estivate - take a long sleep. Nothing's perfect.'

Next Philippa de-slimed Sheldon. Sheldon was a little shocked by the treatment. It *was* rather personal.

'Sheldon, the slime will look too shiny in the photographs. It was best to remove it. You can always excrete some more later for easier gliding down the red carpet.'

Lastly, Philippa led Sheldon to the fake tan room.

'Philippa, I just want a low-level tan because if the UV rays dry me out I'll have to withdraw into my shell.'

Sheldon was now ready for the first photograph. Grandpa Teddy, the ninety-six-year-old fashion model, would be featured in this photograph. A fake shot was lined up with Grandpa using his walker and winning a race against Sheldon the snail.

Sheldon didn't want to say anything but it was rather insulting to assume that an elderly man, direct from physical therapy, could beat him in a race.

'That's the story of my life,' thought Sheldon. 'I admit that I am one of the slowest creatures on the planet but just, occasionally, I'd like to save face.'

Next, Philippa set up a shot where in the foreground Sheldon was lying on a hammock and in the background eight muscle-bound athletes were posing as if they were running an Olympic 100 meters sprint. The caption of the photograph was to be: "A snail's pace for the human race."

Sheldon privately thought that very few humans could slow themselves down, particularly when they feel compelled to answer their smart phones and post pictures of themselves on Facebook every ten seconds.

Philippa, interrupting Sheldon's musings, said, 'Sheldon, we've decided that instead of a still photograph we're going to do a live segment of Celebrity MasterChef. World-renowned Chef Dwayne Brian Smythe is going to make a slow food dish called, "Escargots." That's French for "snails."'

Sheldon beamed. He was delighted that Chef Smythe would produce a delicacy made from his own people.

' . . . So I've now cooked a lovely dish of escargots in parsley butter and garlic. The snails are still in their shells. Just keep the shells stable with your tongs and dig them out with your seafood fork.'

'That's a wrap everybody. Great job.'

Sheldon sat down after the last segment for a break from the fast-moving show. He was more used to moving 0.00758 miles per hour.

One of the television producers glanced over towards Sheldon.

'I think we forgot to put that little fellow in the pot.'

Despite a Herculean attempt to creep away, Sheldon found himself lifted bodily towards the stove and unceremoniously dropped into the broth.

'Oooooh,' he exclaimed. 'I've escaped birds, shrews, mice, worms, hedgehogs, ducks, frogs, toads and snakes to find myself killed by cooking. That's the last time I volunteer for anything. And by the way, I'm not a fan of the slow movement. If I just could have moved a little faster I'd still be alive today.'

'I'm a celebrity . . . Get me out of here.'

THE GAMES

'Ladies and gentlemen, I'd like to welcome you to the five-hundred millionth Amphibian Olympic Games. From the Paleozoic period through today our competitions have united the species and provided role models for millions of frogs, toads, newts and salamanders throughout the planet.'

'I'm Freddie Frog and I'm joined by our commentators Felicia Frog, Teresa Toad and Sidney Salamander. This is the final day of competition. We're going to have an exciting day if the weather holds and we don't need to hibernate.'

'Our first event is the three-metre swim final. This year our youngest competitor is Tony Tadpole, and he's joined by Faith Frog, Felix Frog, Finley Frog, Nicola Newt and Scott Salamander. No toads have entered this event because they generally live on land and they don't have enough practice time.'

(THE GUN GOES OFF.)

'They've shot out of their lanes like bullets,' exclaimed Felicia Frog, winner of the sprint in 2011. 'And look at the size of that webbed hind foot on Felix Frog. Is he another Michael Phelps?'

'Sadly, Freddie, Tony Tadpole doesn't have a prayer of winning even though he's a tough little fellow,' said Sally Salamander. 'He's only just coming into metamorphosis.'

'Yes, Felix Frog is the winner. And now he's pond side with Teresa Toad.'

'How did you feel about that race, Felix?'

'It was rough but I've been working hard on my start and it's really paid off. I'd like to thank my coach and all my supporters back home. I love you, Mum.'

'Truly heartwarming,' said Freddie. 'Now we're going to move on to the wart counting final. The participants are Terence Toad, Tallulah Toad, Tobias Toad, Tessa Toad and Trevor Toad. Each competitor will stand before the judges and be counted.'

(SILENCE DURING JUDGING.)

'The judges have given Terence a 7, Tobias a 7.1,

Tessa a 7.4 and Trevor a huge 8.1. Oh, look, Tallulah has just received a massive 9.4 for 6,207 warts! She has won the competition easily. Teresa is with her now.'

'Teresa, for months I've been drying out my skin and conditioning my poison glands according to a regimen designed by my new coach. My warts clearly stand out from my skin and they're very easy to count.'

'Tallulah, congratulations on an astonishing achievement. We appreciate your talking with us. Good luck at the World Champs next year.'

Freddie announced, 'The next event is the insect swallowing contest. The finalists are Franklin Frog, Fraser Frog, and Nelson Newt. Obviously, the amphibian with the longest and stickiest tongue is predicted to win the event.'

'The gun has just gone off. The competitors are in a screened cage where thousands of beetles, mosquitoes, crickets, gnats, ants, and fruit flies have just been released. The competitors have one hour.'

'Oh, Freddie, it's so exciting,' said Sidney. 'I can see Fraser Frog's eyes sinking into his head to help push a beetle down into his gut.'

'And the winner is . . . Franklin Frog. He swallowed 53 fruit flies in one hour. Normally, it takes him an entire day to eat that many.'

'Absolutely amazing, Freddie. We're in awe of Franklin's prowess.'

'Ladies and gentlemen, it's getting quite warm outside, so we're all going to have a water break and jump into the Olympic-sized pond. For you spectators of other species, we amphibians don't actually drink water. The water will be absorbed by our skins.'

(SHORT PAUSE.)

'Ah, that's better. And now on to the Vocal Challenge Event. Felicia, male frogs and toads will be competing against each other to produce the loudest mating croak.'

'Yes, Freddie, the vocal sacs under their heads blow up and help resonate the sound.'

'The favourites are Tristan, a Natterjack Toad; Fabian, a Puerto Rican Coqui Frog; and Fergus, a Pacific Tree Frog.

'Listen to Fabian, the Coqui Frog,' said Felicia. I think my tympanum has burst. That explosive croak is at least 100 decibels. It's as loud as a pneumatic drill.'

'Yes, Felicia, there's no question that Fabian has won the final and that he will find a mate with that

35

call. What's so unusual is that the Coqui is such a tiny frog. He's only one inch long and weighs just two ounces.'

'Finally, we come to the jumping contest, the most thrilling of all events and the Olympic climax. (ADJUSTING HIS EARPIECE.) Oh, I've just heard from the judges that this competition will be postponed for an hour because the outside temperature is now 107 degrees Fahrenheit, a temperature that causes death to us amphibians.

'That's a shame, Freddie. We were all geared up for the finale.'

'Don't worry, Felicia, the contest will still take place when the sun goes down. Meanwhile, we're going to see a pre-recorded dancing frog exhibition. As you know, dancing frogs live in waterfalls. Waterfalls are so noisy that the females can't hear the male mating calls. So instead, the males attract the females by a dance of stretching and wiggling. Some fans of dancing frogs are proposing that this should be an Olympic event. Let's watch the demonstration now.'

'Freddie,' said Sidney, 'their movements are so eye-catching and athletic. I just love watching them. Their new wiggling routines are especially striking.'

Teresa, microphone in hand, collared Olympic Organizer Lord Ferdinand Frog.

'It's a situation similar to ice dancing years ago when ice dancing was considered inferior to ice skating. These dancing frogs today look pretty and graceful, but is dancing really an Olympic Sport? We'll have to wait and see what the committee thinks.'

'Thank you, Lord Ferdinand. We'll be following dancing frogs in the months to come.'

'OK, everyone, the jumping event is now getting underway. I doubt if the great South African sharp-nosed tree frog Santjie's 1989 record of 33 feet 5.5 inches will be broken today.'

'No, Freddie,' said Sidney. 'I don't think conditions are good enough with such high temperatures. What we really need is for the Cuban Tree Frog to produce his rain call and a thundershower to cool things off.'

'Here goes: Francine Frog starts her jump. (PAUSE.) Oh, no, her jump is only seventeen point five feet. She must be so disappointed; this is way below her personal best; she did have a torn adductor longus on her left hind leg early in the season.'

'Next is Friedrich Frog, world junior champion in 2010. (PAUSE.) He jumps nineteen feet exactly.'

'I don't think Friedrich has really lived up to his

potential after winning the juniors,' remarked Felicia.

'Well, he's still young,' said Sidney. 'This is his first Olympics and he's feeling the pressure.'

Freddie took the microphone. 'Our last competitor is Faisal, a Goliath Frog. (PAUSE.) Now, he jumps. (PAUSE.) Oh my god, it's a massive twenty-seven feet four point seven inches. Well done, Faisal.'

'Ladies and gentlemen, this jump concludes the final event of this year's Amphibian Olympics. Faisal has just received his gold medal and now we'll hear the national anthem of Cameroon. (THE SPECTATORS ARE QUIET.) You can see the tears in Faisal's eyes. It is indeed a magical moment for the Africans.'

'Tune in tomorrow night for the Olympics closing ceremony. The Parade of Nations will be followed by music from Shelby and the Salamanders, tree climbing by South American waxy tree frogs and then, of course, the extinguishing of the Olympic Flame.'

'On behalf of Teresa, Felicia and Sidney and all of us here at Worry Wart Television Studios, thank you for watching and have a good evening.'

JUST A MOTH

I'm just a moth
Living on a tree
Dull and brown
Nothing much to see.

I'm just a moth
Food for bats
Staying away
From dogs and cats.

I'm just a moth
Caterpillar pests
Chew woollen sweaters
Unwelcome houseguests.

I'm just a moth
Flying at night
Cruising the skies
Looking for light.

Melvin the moth was singing a sad song.

'What's wrong with you?' asked Max Moth, his friend.

'I don't want to be a moth anymore. I want to be a butterfly. For one thing, I'm really tired of working at night. I want a day job '

'What's wrong with working at night?'

'It's dark and cold and scary with bats flying about, owls swooping by, and mice jumping towards me.'

'Furthermore, Max, think about sunshine. Butterflies spend much of the day just spreading their wings and getting a suntan.'

'That's because they can't fly unless they're warm.

And we've got the same problem, of course, but instead of basking in sunshine we shiver at night to heat up our wings.'

'I'd still rather be a butterfly,' complained Melvin. 'Butterflies have beautiful wing colours and we're so drab. I'd like to make a fashion statement, too.'

'Looks aren't everything, Melvin.'

'I still think that butterflies have a better deal. Nobody hates a butterfly but plenty of people hate moths. They think that our sole occupation in life is to eat their woollen clothes and carpets. Well, our poor larvae need to eat *something* to keep themselves going.'

'Melvin, people don't hate everything about moths. What about our cousins, the silkworms? Bombyx mori caterpillars cover their cocoons with miles of silk thread which is woven into luxurious fabrics. Everybody likes a silk dressing gown.'

Melvin went home to blend in with a tree trunk.

The next day Max had an idea. 'Melvin, try on this butterfly costume from our drama group and see what happens.'

Melvin put on the butterfly costume and ventured out in the daytime. The first thing he did was land on a beautiful yellow primrose. But as soon as he stuck out his proboscis to drink the nectar, he heard a voice.

'I'm coming to eat you, pretty butterfly,' said Steve the sparrow.

'Uh, oh,' thought Melvin. 'I'd better get out of here fast.'

Melvin flew away and landed this time on some honeysuckle. Then he heard a buzzing sound.

'I'm coming to eat you, pretty butterfly,' said Wally the wasp.

Melvin flew away as fast as mothly possible.

'Hmm, this isn't so easy,' said Melvin. 'And now my wings are tired. I hope I can make it home.'

Melvin stopped for a rest on a lily pad.

'I'm coming to eat you, pretty butterfly,' said Ferdinand the frog.

Melvin shot off that lily pad like nobody's business. Then he went back to the woods to have a drink of rotting apple juice with Max.

'Boy, am I glad to be home. I've learned that butterflies don't have such an easy life. It's not so bad blending in with leaves and drinking tree sap. I'm going to tell my baby caterpillars to accept themselves and not worry about how the other Lepidoptera live.'

Melvin had a new song to sing:

> I'm just a moth
> Spinning silken cocoons
> Doing a job
> By the light of the moon.

I'm just a moth
Pollinating flowers
Jasmine, yucca
I've got the power.

I'm just a moth
To be a butterfly
On second thought
Is more than meets the eye.

I'm just a moth
Not very pretty
Nevertheless
Singing this ditty.

EXPEDITION

'My name is Captain Robert Falcon Scott Rat. I'm here to recruit you for an expedition to Antarctica. As you know, the brown rat population in our country has exploded and we need to find another place to live. No rodents live on the Antarctic continent and we want to set up a new homeland.'

Captain Rat was speaking at a town hall meeting. This expedition was quite a daring idea for the community of brown rats, most of whom stay close to their homes in sewers, buildings, warehouses, public tips, shops, restaurants and supermarkets.

'We need weather-rats, fisher-rats, builders, carpenters, sledge drivers, dentists, and logistics personnel. We need men, women and children for our new colony. Who wants to escape the rat race and come along on the adventure of a lifetime?'

Hundreds of rats squeaked, 'Yes.' Captain Rat was surprised and delighted at their enthusiasm. However, one big brown rat called Ralph stood up.

'Why do you think we will succeed when so many other expeditions have failed? We don't want to die out there in the extreme cold away from our friends and families.'

'The reason is, Ralph, that we will be prepared. We have learned lessons from the past and we know what we need to do. For example, we know that human skin can freeze in sixty seconds. Our own hairless tails are at risk so we will design and manufacture tailcoats, as well as rat goggles and rat gloves.'

'That's fine, Captain, but where will we live? We need stability because many of us lost our homes in the Christchurch earthquake not too long ago.'

'My plan is to live in the McMurdo research station along side the human population. Because one pair of brown rats can produce 15,000 descendants in one year, we can dig holes down to the permafrost or build igloos for additional housing. Our front claws are well-adapted to digging and our incisors can cut blocks of ice.'

'What about food?'

'Our main source of food would be the scraps that the research scientists throw away.   But we can also eat wingless midges, lichen and moss.   We can fish. We might get our digits on some Penguin eggs and even some Penguin chicks.'

'That sounds pretty tasty.'

'Great. Anyone who wants to go, please put a paw print on the list at the back of the hall.'

And so the great expedition began.   Captain Rat's plan was to stow away on the tourist ship, "Spirit of Enderby," anchored at Lyttelton, New Zealand and travel south through the Southern Ocean and the Ross Sea to Antarctica.   They would leave early in the summer month of December.

In the dead of night the pack of three hundred rats and one hundred mice labourers ran across the ropes to hide in the hold. The ship embarked the next day.

Walter Weather-Rat came up to see Captain Rat on the second day of the journey.

'I think we're in for some stormy seas,' he said, looking around. 'I see some pretty seasick rats, Captain.'

'Ask Doctor Rat to poach some anti-seasickness tablets from the ship's sickbay.'

Most of their party got their sea legs in a few days. The excitement started straightaway.

'Oh, look at the seal pups,' cried Rebecca Rat, one of the mother-rats. 'Aren't they adorable?'

'Do you see the humpback whales?' said Ralph Rat.

Then on the horizon Captain Rat and his first mate, Ronald Rat, spotted an iceberg.

Ronald said, 'That iceberg is half the size of Greater London. It's heading right this way. If it hits the ship, we've had it.'

Some of the rats started screaming and some of them said their prayers. Fortunately, the ship swerved out of its way.

A little later Ralph Rat wept, 'Oh, I've got to see Dentist Rat. I've got terrible toothache.'

Because there was so little to gnaw on the ship, the Ralph's incisors became overgrown and he could no longer eat; the incisors started growing into the roof of his mouth. Dentist Rat had to file off the edges.

After a wretched journey onboard ship they arrived at Ross Island next to the Ross Ice Shelf. Now the group had to get to the research station. The twenty carpenters built tiny sledges out of compressed rat droppings. The sledge drivers harnessed the mice to pull the sleds and yelled, 'Mush.' The mice started running.

'Oh, my, it is cold,' said Rebecca Rat. 'I'm about to give birth to my litter and I'm worried that they'll freeze. After all, they'll be blind, hairless and helpless.'

Captain Rat reassured her, 'Don't worry, Rebecca. We'll all huddle together and keep warm.'

Later on the whole party gathered together for a rest. Captain Rat suggested, 'Let's have some entertainment. How about some dancing? What about the scene from the Nutcracker ballet where the nutcracker leads his troops into a fierce battle against the rats?'

Immediately some toddler rats stood up and glided on the ice. Their mothers and fathers blew them kisses and took ratographs.

The day finally came when the troop arrived at their destination. There were squeals of joy from the entire pack.

'What a fantastic achievement, everyone. I congratulate all of you.'

'For he's a jolly good fellow,' was sung to Captain Rat.

Everyone sat down for a nice meal of potato peelings. As they were eating, one thin, bedraggled brown rat limped over to their party.

Captain Rat said, 'We're delighted to see you, sir. We're here to start a new rat colony in Antarctica.'

'I'm Richard Rat. I've must tell you that the situation here is not good. We came aboard a cruise ship to Campbell Island in the sub-Antarctic but we ran out of food. We found several avian varieties of teal, snipe and pipits. Unfortunately, we ate them all. Then we tried to find other nesting birds but they're becoming extinct, too. The worst thing is that humans have begun a rodent extermination project and most of us have died eating rat poison. I just floated along the currents and landed here. If I were you, I'd go home as soon as possible.'

All the rats looked at each other. Go home? What a crazy idea!

The pack settled into life in Antarctica. Their accommodation in the research station's basement and drains was very comfortable and they found plenty to eat in the rubbish bins.

Ralph Rat remarked, 'I don't know what I was so worried about. Everything has gone very smoothly, just like Captain Rat said.'

Rebecca, the mother-rat, added, 'This is a great

place for our children to play and grow up.'

However, a few weeks later the rats felt a sudden drop in temperature. Even though it was summer, the thermometer dropped to minus twenty degrees centigrade and a blizzard raged outside. Everyone was shivering and some of the newborns looked frozen.

'What does everyone think?' asked Captain Rat. 'Should we go or should we stay?'

Dentist Rat talked about the good points: 'We've got clean, fresh air. We've got shelter in the basement of the research station. We've brought new rats into the world. We have enough food at the moment.'

Ralph Rat said, 'I think you're forgetting that now it's summer. The temperature could go down to minus fifty degrees centigrade in the winter. Our rat population is increasing and we could run out of food scraps. We won't be able to go outside at all. Can we really see ourselves stuck in that basement for six months of the year?'

Rebecca sobbed, 'Some of our babies are very frail. I miss my family and I miss RatGrocers. I need some ratsitting help with my children and it's much easier to get food back home.'

Captain Rat asked his first mate, 'Are there any ships leaving soon?'

'Yes, the "Orion" is leaving in early March. You'd just have time to make it to the port before winter sets in.'

'Let's have a vote,' said the Captain. 'Raise your paws if you want to go home.'

Forty-four thousand one hundred twenty-nine paws were raised in favour. Thirty-three thousand four hundred seventy-one paws were against.

'We're going home!' rejoiced Rebecca.

All the rats gathered up their belonging and made their way to the sledges. The mice were hitched and drivers shouted, 'Mush.'

Doctor Rat spoke to Captain Rat. 'You've definitely made the right decision. I'm relieved to go home before too many rats go hungry or perish from the cold.'

The Captain replied, 'I wanted to be the first leader of rats to colonize a new continent. I wanted to go down in ratstory as a great explorer and fly the Ratland flag. I wanted to invoke the credo of that other Robert Falcon Scott who went to the South Pole in 1912: 'To strive, to seek, to find, and not to yield.' I guess it just wasn't meant to be.'

'Cheer up, Captain. Once we're home you can stow away on the next mission to the International

Space Station.'

BIRTHDAY

It was Gordon Gorilla's tenth birthday party. All twenty members of his family were gathered in a clearing in the forest near the Virunga volcanoes in

Central Africa. They were eating a birthday meal of wild celery, thistles and bamboo shoots.

Gordon looked around and said, 'Where's Dad?'

'Look over there,' said Mum.

A huge, silverback gorilla walked to the clearing on his knuckles and then stood up and roared, beat his chest, and bared his gigantic canine teeth.

'Dad, you're really scaring me,' said Gordon.

'Get out, Gordon. Leave the family. We can't see you ever again.'

'But, Dad, I don't understand. Why are you sending me away?'

'You're a silverback - a grown gorilla - and you need a family of your own. You can't mate with your own mother or sisters. Go make your own way in the world.'

So on that dreadful birthday Gordon went off, all

by himself, to the other side of the mountain.

It was a sad, lonely life for Gordon. Every day had the same routine: eating, digesting and resting; eating, digesting and resting; and moving to a new sleeping nest each night. He missed his wrestling with his baby brothers and sisters after the morning meal and he missed talking to his parents and siblings.

After a year of wandering the forest alone, Gordon met a group of three male, mountain gorillas.

'You're the first gorillas I've met since I was thrown out of the family,' he said.

'We were all pushed out of our families,' said one of the strangers.

'How has it been for you?' asked Gordon.

'The worst thing has been the poachers,' replied Gilbert, the largest of the silverbacks. 'I think they really want to catch antelope but Gerry walked right into a snare. We were able to dismantle the wire, but his hand was amputated. Thank goodness he's OK now. How about you?'

'I saw some humans grazing their cattle in our homeland. They cut down trees for firewood. Pretty soon we gorillas will have nowhere to live.'

'It's very worrying for all of us.'

Then Gordon asked, 'Have you seen any available females?'

'No, only in family groups. We had to stay away because the dominant male gorillas looked very healthy and dangerous to us.'

Gilbert then suggested, 'Gordon, would you like to join our little group?'

Gordon answered, 'I would be delighted.'

Gordon spent two years with the three males,

Gilbert, Gerry and Guy. They foraged for meals together - they each needed to eat about thirty kilograms of food each day. Fortunately, food was plentiful in the forests. From January to August they moved to the higher ground of the Hagenia forests and ate the leaves, stems, flowers and berries of the Gallium vines. Sometimes they used rocks to smash open palm nuts. Every night each gorilla built a platform of stems, twigs, leaves and branches by twisting, knotting and weaving the pieces together; they never used the same sleeping nest twice.

One day the little group came upon a family of gorillas on the mountainside. They hid behind some moss-covered trees and studied the situation. There were several females, some young male blackback gorillas, five juveniles and three babies. The leader of the group was a tall silverback but he was very frail and thin. Gordon guessed it was because his teeth had worn down over the years and he wasn't able to eat. Guy thought he might have caught a human respiratory disease when tourists came to observe the gorillas. Gilbert, the largest gorilla in their male group, decided to try his luck and push out the old silverback.

Gordon said, 'I'd be careful if I were you. That old boy might have a lot of muscle still in him.'

Gilbert plunged right in and walked over to the group. The old leader opened his mouth, bared his teeth, screamed, and roared with all his might. When he beat his chest the 'pok-pok' noises could be heard over a kilometre away. Gilbert, however, bit him on the neck and face with his sharp, canine teeth, picked up sticks, pulled branches and then broke the elderly gorilla's arm bones. The old ape ran away from his family who hooted a bark of alarm.

Gordon observed Gilbert's victory, 'You've got your own family now, Gilbert. I'm very jealous.'

'You just need to be bold,' encouraged Gilbert. 'The next thing I have to do is kill all the babies in the family. I have to ensure that I am the father of all the youngsters in my group.'

Although this was how Mother Nature ensured survival of the species, it was a harsh way of life. Gordon, Gerry and Guy departed the scene.

The three of them spent another year on the mountain. At the end of that year, two terrible things happened: Guy was killed by stepping on a land mine left from the civil war in Rwanda and Gerry was killed for bushmeat by illegal hunters.

Gordon was sad and lonely again. He was back to his old routine of eating, digesting and resting;

eating, digesting and resting, and moving to a new sleeping nest each night.

'What do I have to live for?' lamented Gordon. 'I've no family and no friends. The mountains are a hostile habitat. What am I to do?'

At that very moment of despair, Gordon sniffed something in the air. It was the fragrance of a female gorilla ready to mate. He followed the scent and found, much to his surprise, a single, female mountain gorilla. Even though he was very shy Gordon wandered over to make her acquaintance.

'Hello. I'm Gordon Gorilla.'

'Pleased to meet you, Gordon, I'm Grace Gorilla. Do you come here often?'

'No, I'm new in town.'

'Well, let me show you around,' said Grace. 'Here are some tender bamboo shoots and here is some wild celery.'

'Oh, I used to eat a lot of wild celery with my birth family,' said Gordon.

'Me, too. I miss everything I used to do with mine. When I was eight years old my father made me leave my family. He said that to avoid inbreeding I had to mate with a male outside my family group and bring up children with him.'

'I suppose you felt very hurt and lonely when he said that. I know I did.'

Grace nodded, 'You are a very sensitive and understanding silverback. I'd like to get to know you better.'

Gordon belched a big noise of happiness. 'I would love to know you too, Grace. And in a little while, perhaps we could mate and raise our own family. I'll care for you and protect you and the children for as many years as I can.'

Grace broke the silence between them with a happy chirp. 'But first, how about a drink of rainwater caught in our fur? Then we can do something about supper.'

'Great idea,' said Gordon.

Gordon and Grace walked together out of the clearing and into the sunset. They headed up the mountain.

FEATHEREX

'Okay, everyone, we're a little late with our deliveries today. Check the warehouse for any last minute requests.'

Conrad Carrier Pigeon, manager of Feather Express, was determined to deliver every letter and parcel on time, wherever and whenever they were needed.

Conrad scanned a list to see which members of his team were in today. First, he had Peregrine "Lightning" Falcon, who swoops at 322 kilometres per hour. Then he had Lucy Lovebird who transports delicate items in her tail feathers, Oliver Owl who works in darkness, and Stefan Stork who carries babies. Conrad's able assistant and right-hand bird, Carolina, another Carrier Pigeon, was also on staff today. Arnold Albatross was off with a wounded wing.

Conrad listened to the news for a few moments. The Flyraq war was escalating. Flyraq had been at peace only a few years when migrating Flocks started a violent civil war with the Gaggles. Getting parcels through Flyraq war zones would be a huge challenge for FeatherEx.

Today's first task was to deliver a letter from Elliot Egret in Flyraq to his family, letting them know that he was alive and well. His letter read:

> **Dear Mum and Dad,**
>
> **I miss you very much. The fighting is frightening and many of my friends are missing, but I am fine and my studies are going well. I'll come home just as soon as I can. Please try not to worry. Your loving son,**
>
> **Elliot**

Conrad thought that it would be so wonderful to have a son as thoughtful and affectionate as Elliot; he was always so busy at FeatherEx that he had never had time for a wife or children.

Conrad gave the letter to Carolina for delivery.

Carolina said, 'I'll do my best to reassure Elliot's family. I'm sure I can make the delivery today and be back at headquarters by teatime. Remember our motto: Delivery in fair weather or fowl.' Carolina took off into the sky.

After that FeatherEx had to transmit a coded message from General Emu in Fowlbury to the Prime Minister in Birdseedham, updating him on the status of the fighting. General Emu's message reported:

Problems on the ground. Snipes killing our soldiers. No worms, no seeds, no insects.

'What a worry for the Prime Minister,' exclaimed Conrad, who desperately wanted to help the soldiers to end the war. Conrad asked Lightning to transport the secret message. Then he sent the FeatherEx Pelican Division to Fowlbury with birdseed and fat balls.   Lucy   Lovebird   would   transport   juicy earthworms.

Next FeatherEx needed to deliver a letter from Gladys to Gary.   These two were sweetheart Goldcrests since they fledged, but Gladys's family had moved from Duckdale to Geeseglen right before the war started so that Gladys's father could get a better job in the oil industry. Now their two families were on opposing sides of the conflict. None of this mattered to Gladys and Gary. They just wanted to get married.

> **Dearest Gary,**
>
> **I love you with all my heart. I miss you every day. Mother and Father tell me to forget about you but I never will. I want to get through enemy lines and come back to you.**
>
> **All my love,**
>
> **Gladys**

Conrad was in tears after reading this letter. He knew all about loneliness. He *had* to help Gladys get to Gary. There must be a way; after all, a Goldcrest is a tiny songbird that weighs only about six grams.

Conrad worried and fretted all day. Late in the afternoon he talked to Carolina who had just returned from delivering Elliot Egret's message to his family.

Carolina said, 'Of course, why didn't I think of this sooner? Let's have Oliver Owl take her in his talons tonight when there's no moon and the soldiers won't be able to see them. We can ask him to get her false papers and a false identification ring.'

Conrad agreed, 'Carolina, that's a brilliant solution. I'll get Oliver on the case right away.'

After a hectic day, Conrad just wanted to put his claws up and rest for a few moments but there was one more package to deliver. A baby cuckoo called,

"Caitlin," only two days old, was abandoned when her mother and father were killed in the Eastern war zone. She had no family anywhere; without urgent care she would perish. The birdcall network was down because of the war so Conrad couldn't contact social services. He made a snap decision. He decided that he, Conrad, would adopt baby Caitlin. He asked Stefan Stork to pick up Caitlin and bring her to Conrad's officenest.

Stefan Stork set off on the rescue trip. The skies were full of dense smoke from all the bombing and he could barely find his way. He flew directly into the path of a Skyhawk Avian A4D which, fortunately, steered away from Stefan's flight path at the last minute. Then he flew over the Capitolnest where gunmen were firing suet pellets into the air. Stefan was very frightened. He kept repeating FeatherEx's mantra: Delivery in fair weather or fowl . . . delivery in fair weather or fowl . . . delivery in fair weather or fowl. Somehow Stefan remained calm and made it to the Eastern war zone where he picked up Caitlin.

Conrad was pacing when Stefan showed up with the baby. Carolina was there, too. They both cooed at the baby and fed her some choice spiders. As happy as he was to see baby Caitlin, Conrad suddenly turned towards his assistant, Carolina, and realized that she was always there for him: she helped him with every delivery and in every crisis.

Conrad said, 'Carolina, you are the heart and soul of Feather Express and the love of my life. Will you marry me and help me bring up Caitlin?'

Carolina responded, 'Of course I will, Conrad. I love and respect you more than any Carrier Pigeon I have ever known.'

* * *

It was a tough day for FeatherEx but they pride themselves on managing tough jobs. They are willing to accept the extreme delivery challenges of wartime. At the end of this demanding twenty-four hours, the team stood united and sang the company song:

> We're Feather Express
> Air transport success
> Never throw in the towel
> Delivery in fair weather or fowl.

THE PAGEANT

'Good evening and welcome vertebrates, arthropods and molluscs to the 2015 Miss Animal Kingdom Pageant. Tonight, you'll meet all the contestants as they parade down the runway and then we will announce the five finalists. Get ready for a

79

wonderful evening of beauty, poise and intelligence,' announced Reginald Rhinoceros, master of ceremonies.

'This year's contestants are the most attractive and talented that we've seen in many years,' added Camilla Coyote, co-host and runner-up in 1998.

(PAGEANT THEME MUSIC BEGINS. EACH CONTESTANT WALKS DOWN THE AISLE).

'Now,' said Reginald, 'Let us introduce you to all our competitors:'

> Miss Carol Condor from California
> Miss Vanessa Vampire Bat from Mexico
> Miss Tallulah Tropical Orb Spider from
>   Venezuela
> Miss Nancy Natterjack Toad from East Anglia,
>   Great Britain
> Miss Andrea African Egg-Eating Snake from
>   Southern Africa
> Miss Irene Iguana from the Galapagos Islands
> Miss Wanda Warthog from Botswana
> Miss Charlotte Coconut Crab from
>   Madagascar
> Miss Florence Flea from Brooklyn, New York

and, finally,
Miss Tabitha Tasmanian Devil from
Tasmania.'

'Let's hear it for this years contestants. (LOUD CLAPPING.) Judging was extremely difficult but our experts have finally come to an agreement. So there's no time like the present to announce our five finalists. The envelope, please.'

'Our finalists are:

Miss Tallulah Tropical Orb Spider
Miss Vanessa Vampire Bat
Miss Andrea African Egg-Eating Snake
Miss Florence Flea and
Miss Tabitha Tasmanian Devil.'

(DELIGHTED SQUEALS FROM THE FINALISTS)

'We'll be right back after a word from our sponsors.'

'Now it's time for the talent segment of the competition. Our first contestant is Tallulah, Miss Tropical Orb Spider. She is a student at Central Rainforest University, studying Advanced Web Design with a minor in Edible Insects. Tonight she is weaving a web for catching moths.'

'OMG, her web is finished and its circumference is a massive 5.7 metres. Well done, Tallulah.'

'Reginald, the audience is on its feet. They are amazed at this prodigious talent.'

'Yes, Camilla, Tallulah is a wonderful example of

the talent here tonight. Now, let's move on to our second finalist, Miss Vanessa Vampire Bat, a Veterinary Medicine student. Tonight she is going to make a small cut on a pig and suck out the blood. Pablo Pig has volunteered to assist Vanessa in her talent demonstration.'

'We're now going to turn off the lights in the auditorium because Vanessa only works at night. (WHISPERING). Now, audience, notice that Vanessa has made a small cut on the sleeping pig and has licked the wound. Pablo hasn't even woken up because the bite is hardly noticeable.'

'Look: Vanessa is sucking the blood.'

'Now: Vanessa has just finished and is flying back to her roost. Pablo is still asleep.'

'Reginald, that was an amazing demonstration. We've seen Dracula films, but I've never before seen a live vampire bat in action.'

'Yes, Camilla, Vanessa is an extremely accomplished bat and a credit to her Desmodontinae family.'

'Our next finalist is Miss Andrea African Egg-Eating Snake. Andrea is going to eat a Weaver Bird's egg which is three times the size of her head. In place of teeth Andrea has thick folds of muscular gum tissue. The folds are like suction cups that pull the egg steadily into her mouth. Once the egg is in her throat, sharp projections from her backbone pierce the shell and the liquid goes into her belly. Then she regurgitates the shell, all in one piece.'

'Reginald, Andrea is a marvel of nature. What a talent!'

'Our fourth finalist is Miss Florence Flea who is studying Parasitology. Florence is going to display her jumping skills. Just to put it in perspective, fleas can jump up to 200 times their height. This is equivalent to a human jumping the Empire State Building in New York. So now Florence is going to jump straight from the ground on to our volunteer, Carlton the Cat.'

'Reginald, it's another awesome arthropod talent. Well done, Florence.'

'Finally, our last talent contestant is Miss Tabitha Tasmanian Devil. She is going to eat a whole chicken, including feathers, bones, intestines and flesh.'

'What a powerhouse, Reginald. She doesn't care what she eats and likes dead animals as well as live ones.'

'Ladies and gentlemen, that's the conclusion of the talent competition. When we return we'll speak to each of our finalists.'

> **Instinctive Cosmetics**: If you're not happy with your appearance, call 800-ANA-TOMY. We offer every kind of cosmetic surgery from tentacle to claw. Our speciality is fur colouring. Let Instinctive Cosmetics transform your life.

'Our five finalists are on stage now for their interviews. Question One to Miss Tropical Orb Spider: What do you wish for?'

'Reginald, the answer is, as always, "world peace." Today we have lions fighting warthogs, gazelles fighting baboons, robins fighting caterpillars. History keeps repeating itself. We never seem to learn from our past and the fighting never ends.'

'Question Two to Miss African Egg-Eating Snake: 'How do you measure success?'

'Reginald, as long as we work towards achieving

our goals and help other members of our Animal Kingdom, we are *all* winners.'

'Thank you, Andrea. Question three to Miss Vampire Bat: How do you respond to people who say that the pageant is outdated and feminist and who want, instead, glamour and airheads?'

Before Andrea had a chance to answer, there was a quick kerfuffle on stage. Miss Tallulah Tropical Orb Spider trapped Miss Florence Flea in her magnificent web and ate her.

Reginald announced to the audience, 'Ladies and gentlemen, I'm sorry to report Florence's death. However, the show must go on. Miss Vampire Bat, are you all right to continue?'

'Yes, Reginald. I'd say to the pageant critics who prefer glamour and airheads that you might not like how we look but we can't change our outward appearances. We all can't be tigers or peacocks or butterflies. But we think we have something far more important: we are women who want to make a difference.'

'That was a humble and touching answer,' said Camilla.

'And now our last question to Miss Tabitha, Tasmanian Devil: What do you think is the biggest problem of our youth today?'

'The youth of today have all the problems of jobs, housing and education that the animal kingdom has always had. But the youth of today have one additional problem: technology. We all have to put away our phones and tablets and play stations and get involved with real life, creating a better world to live in.'

'Ladies, your answers have been marvelous.

We'll have a short break while the judges confer on their decision. Camilla, whom do you think the judges will choose?'

'It's a tough one, Reginald. All the girls have striking looks and exceptional talent, and they all have thought through some of the pressing issues of our day.'

'I agree, Camilla, it's impossible to say. Oh, I see that the judges have made their decision. May I have the envelope, please? And the winner is . . .'

(DRUM ROLL)

'Vanessa, Miss Vampire Bat. I crown you 'Miss Animal Kingdom 2015.' Vanessa, your beauty, charm and talent have graced our stage this week. We salute you as our next Miss Animal Kingdom and we wish you happiness and success in your reign.'

(PAGEANT
THEME SONG)

She's Miss Animal Kingdom
And don't you agree
She's got poise, talent
And personality.

Fur or scales
Wings or membrane
Feathers or talons
She's not a bird brain.

Phylum, class
Beauty or grotesque
Genus, species
Of scientific interest.

She's Miss Animal Kingdom
Youth at its best
Not just a pretty face
She's really passed the test.

ABOUT THE AUTHOR

Lynn Blake John grew up in Washington, DC and lives in Carmarthen, Wales. She was an IT geek in her day job. Nowadays, she works as an artist, writer, illustrator, and art teacher. She uses all media and particularly likes the odd and humorous effects that can be achieved with collage. Some of her recent projects include an exhibition of the strange beauty of seedpods at the National Botanical Gardens of Wales, 'Revenge of the Vegetables,' (for kids who won't eat their greens), 'The Accidental Athlete' (for kids who won't exercise) and the 'Animal Chronicles.' She loves teaching and has a Master's degree in Education.

Printed in Great Britain
by Amazon

33608983R00056